Two Plus One Goes A.P.E.

Two Plus One Goes A.P.E.

by Tricia Springstubb

Illustrated by Nancy Poydar

A
LITTLE APPLE
PAPERBACK

SCHOLASTIC INC.

New York   Toronto   London   Auckland   Sydney

No part of this publication may be reproduced in whole or in part, or
stored in a retrieval system, or transmitted in any form or by any means,
electronic, mechanical, photocopying, recording, or otherwise, without
written permission of the publisher. For information regarding
permission, write to Scholastic Inc., 555 Broadway, New York, NY 10012.

ISBN 0-590-25243-7

Text copyright © 1995 by Tricia Springstubb.
Illustrations copyright © 1995 by Scholastic Inc.
All rights reserved. Published by Scholastic Inc.
APPLE PAPERBACKS is a registered trademark of Scholastic Inc.

12 11 10 9 8 7 6 5 4 3 2 1   5 6 7 8 9/9 0/0

Printed in the U.S.A.   40

First Scholastic printing, April 1995

3354 0169 4-08

For the children of Coventry School,
and for the staff,
who "make a difference" every day

contents

1

The Most Wonderful Place in the World

Betsy Jones charged across the playground.

"I've got an itch as big as New Jersey!" she shouted.

Betsy ran all the way to the old willow tree. She leaned against it and rubbed her shoulders up and down, up and down.

The bark was bumpy and rough.

"Aaaah," she sighed. "That feels better."

Her best friend, Ida Rose, started laughing. "Are you crazy?" she asked.

"This tree is the world's best back-scratcher," said Betsy. "Aaah!"

The playground was boiling hot. The willow tree was the only shade.

"I'm about to melt," Ida said. Her plump face was red and shiny.

"Come under my tree," said Betsy. "In the nice, cool shade."

"It's not your tree," said Ida. "It's the whole school's tree."

"I know, I know," said Betsy.

Ida was right, as usual.

Still, Betsy thought. *Nobody loves this old tree as much as I do*.

"Hi, Betsy! Hi, Ida!" Missy Mason ran by. Her hair was sticking up all over the place, as usual. She put a Frisbee on her head.

"Like my new sun visor?" she asked.

"Weird," said Ida.

"Smart," said Betsy.

"Recess ends in two minutes," said Ida. "Come play wild ponies."

Ida galloped away. Her long, beautiful hair tossed exactly like a pony's mane.

But Betsy stayed under the willow. Its trunk was wide and sturdy. Its branches were yellow as gold.

The branches bent almost to the ground. They made a little golden room all around the trunk.

Betsy closed her eyes.

This was her favorite spot in the world.

"Be-e-e-e-etsy!" hollered Ida.

Betsy's eyes flew open.

"Bye, tree," she whispered. "See you to-morrow, same time, same place!"

Then she pawed the ground. "Neigh!" she cried, exactly like a wild pony, and galloped toward her friend.

2

Going A.P.E.

Back inside, Mrs. Myer let everybody get a drink.

"I feel like a flapjack on the griddle," said P.J. Smith.

"I know it's hot," Mrs. Myer said, "but please settle down. When everyone is quiet we can talk about our big project."

Ida stood up. She put her finger to her lips.

"SSSHHH!" She sounded like a giant balloon losing its air.

Betsy laughed.

"Betsy Jones!" said Mrs. Myer, raising a finger.

Betsy slid down in her seat. She looked out the window at the willow tree. Its branches waved at her. Just looking at the tree made her feel cooler.

"Earth Day is coming soon," said Mrs. Myer. "For our class project, we are each going to adopt a patch of earth."

"I don't get it," said Tyler Brown.

"Me either," said Erin Lucky.

"I feel like a fried egg," said P.J. Smith.

"SSSHHH!" said Ida again.

"Tonight when you go home, look around your neighborhood," said Mrs. Myer. "Find a little patch of earth that needs some T.L.C."

"That stands for Tender Loving Care," explained Ida.

"That's right, Ida." Mrs. Myer smiled. "Maybe you'll find an empty lot where nothing grows. Or a place people litter."

"I know a corner like that," said Tyler.

"You can adopt it," said Mrs. Myer. "You can clean it up."

"He can put up a giant sign that says DON'T LITTER," said Ida.

"Great," said Mrs. Myer.

"I could plant some flowers," said Tyler. "My mom has seeds."

"Excellent!" said Mrs. Myer.

"I know!" cried Ida. "We can call it A.P.E., for Adopt a Piece of Earth!"

"The A.P.E. project!" said Mrs. Myer. "I like that!"

Now everybody started talking at once.

Betsy felt excited. She loved taking care of things. And she knew exactly what piece of earth she wanted to adopt. There was no question in her mind.

But there was a problem.

Her spot wasn't junky. And something already grew there. Still, she wanted to take care of it more than anyplace else in the world.

"Hey, look at the hard hats!" Erin pointed out the window.

A man and a woman in yellow hats were walking around outside. They were staring up at the willow.

"What are they doing, Mrs. Myer?" Betsy asked.

"I'm not sure. We'll find out later. Boys and girls, tonight's homework is to draw a picture of your patch of earth. In a week or so, we'll draw another picture. We'll see how things have changed."

Then Mrs. Myer held up one finger. Her mouth made a shape like an egg.

Betsy knew she was going to say *something important*.

"Remember, boys and girls," said Mrs. Myer. "*You* can make a difference."

"Can we go out and see what those workers are doing?" asked Erin.

"Not now," said Mrs. Myer. "We have to line up for gym."

"Gym!" howled P.J. "I'm already as hot as popcorn in the popper!"

In gym they did jumping jacks. Instead of counting "1-2-3-4," Betsy whispered, "My-spe-cial-place!"

When they got back to their room, the workers were gone.

But Betsy's willow tree was still there, as beautiful as ever.

3

Not the
Haunted House!

After school Betsy, Ida, and Missy walked home together.

Missy was one year younger. She was in a different class.

Today it was taking a million years to get home, because Missy kept stopping to pick up bugs. She was putting them in her lunch box. She planned to make a bug village when she got home.

"Betsy and I have a special project to do, Missy," said Ida. "We don't have time to waste."

"Uno momento," said Missy. She lifted a rock. Round gray bugs started running for their lives.

"Gross me out," said Ida and marched up the street.

Betsy ran after her.

"Do you know what you're doing for your special project?" she asked Ida.

Ida smiled and pointed across the street.

"There it is," she said.

Betsy gasped. "Not the haunted house!"

The haunted house was dark and gloomy. It had a broken-down porch and dirty windows with torn curtains. The yard was full of tall weeds. Tucked in the weeds were old candy wrappers and rusty cans.

Nobody had lived there as long as they could remember. Nobody ever, ever went near it.

"If anyplace needs T.L.C., it's that place," said Ida.

"But . . . people say there are bones in the basement! And bats and . . . and . . ."

Missy came running up. She opened her lunch box.

"Six carpenter ants, three worms, eighteen potato bugs . . ."

"If you don't mind," said Ida, "Betsy and I are discussing our A.P.E. project."

"We're supposed to find a patch of earth and take care of it," Betsy explained.

"Cool," said Missy. "Find a spot with lots of bugs."

Ida put her hands on her hips.

"F.Y.I., which means For Your Information, I'm adopting the haunted house," she said.

Missy sucked in her breath. "You are?"

"Yes, I am."

"Wooeee," Missy whispered. "I'll bet the spiders in there are as big as bathtubs."

Ida looked a little sick. She really did not like bugs. "Who cares?" she said. "If anyplace needs T.L.C., it's the haunted house."

"Bets, what are you going to do?" Missy asked.

Betsy rubbed the toe of her shoe in the dirt.

She coughed.

Maybe she should change her mind.

Probably she should.

But she said, "I want to take care of the willow tree at school."

"Sweet," said Missy. "I love that tree."

"That doesn't make sense," said Ida. "That tree is fine. It doesn't need you."

"I know," said Betsy. "But . . . well, it's my favorite tree on earth."

Ida tossed her hair.

"It's up to you," she said. "I have to go. *My* project is going to take a huge amount of *really* hard work!"

She marched away.

"What a show-off," said Missy.

She patted Betsy's arm.

"Let's make sugar sandwiches at my house," she said.

The sugar sandwiches were delicious.

The carpenter ants thought so, too.

14

Still Betsy felt bad.

Ida was right, as usual. Betsy's project didn't make sense.

It was dumb.

And she still wanted to do it.

Could that mean she was dumb, too?

4

Excellent!

In school the next day, Mrs. Myer hung up everyone's drawings.

Tyler was adopting his bus stop.

Erin was adopting the alley next to her apartment.

P.J. was adopting his grandmother's garden, since his grandmother wasn't feeling well lately.

No one could believe Ida was adopting the haunted house.

Her picture was done with lots of black

and red. It made the haunted house look even spookier than it was.

She tossed her long hair. She did a little twirl.

"Wait till you see it a week from now," she said. "It'll be so beautiful, you won't recognize it!"

"Betsy Jones, where's your picture?" Mrs. Myer asked.

Betsy reached in her desk.

She had worked hard on the picture. It had come out just the way she wanted, not one mess up.

Too bad Mrs. Myer was going to tell her it was a dumb idea.

"What a beautiful drawing," said Mrs. Myer. "I can tell you love this tree! Where is it?"

Betsy's face grew hot. She pointed out the window.

"The playground tree?" asked Mrs. Myer.

Everyone was looking at Betsy. Her face felt as hot as a three-alarm fire.

"You think that tree is special?" asked Mrs. Myer.

Betsy was so embarrassed, all she could do was nod.

"Excellent!" said Mrs. Myer.

"Uh . . . excellent?"

"Most of us take that tree for granted," said Mrs. Myer. "You can help us see why it's special. Will you do that, Betsy?"

"Yes!" Betsy punched the air with her fist.

Everybody started doing the same thing. "Yes! Yes!"

At recess Betsy ran straight to the willow.

She rubbed her back against it, up and down, up and down.

Then she sat under it and looked up.

The leaves were just coming out. They were long and pointy, like little silver fish.

In the breeze the branches made a silky,

swooshing sound. One brushed her shoulder, as if to tell her something.

"Good idea," said Betsy.

She picked up a thin branch that had fallen on the ground. She wound it around her arm like a golden bracelet.

Missy Mason ran by with a caterpillar draped across her pointy little nose.

"You look cozy!" she yelled. "Cozy as a bird in a nest!"

"You got it," said Betsy.

5

Frankenstein

After school Betsy's big sister Julia took her to the library.

Julia read books on How to Speak Japanese, How to Become a TV News-caster, and How to Have a Big Wardrobe on a Tiny Budget.

Betsy read about trees.

She couldn't believe how many different kinds there were.

There was no such thing as a maple tree.

There were silver maples, sugar maples, Norway maples, Japanese maples.

No such thing as a willow.

There were weeping willows, black willows, furry willows, silky willows, and prairie willows. Not to mention pussy willows.

Mrs. Myer was right. Most people did take trees for granted.

But not the Native Americans.

Betsy read that they believed each tree had its own soul.

One tree wasn't like another tree, anymore than one person was like another.

I think so, too, Betsy said to herself.

Betsy copied down as many amazing facts as she could. She wrote until her hand started to hurt. Then she and Julia walked home.

When they got to the haunted house, they stopped.

Ida was in the front yard. Her hair was wild. Her face was covered with green streaks.

She looked like someone who might live in the haunted house.

"What's so interesting?" she asked crossly.

She waved a pair of grass clippers. The sharp blades glinted in the sun.

"Wh-what are you doing with those?" asked Betsy.

"My mother won't let me use the lawn mower," Ida said. "So I'm cutting the grass with these."

"Oh!" said Betsy. "But that will take all day!"

"No, it won't," said Ida. "It will take all *week*! I've been working for two hours and this is all I did."

Ida wiped her plump, greenish-red face.

"Take a break," said Julia. "Come over for some Kool-Aid."

"I'd tell you to M.Y.O.B., which means Mind Your Own Business," said Ida. "Only Betsy is my best friend."

She tossed her hair.

Then she screamed.

"Eeek! A bug's on me!"

"It's just a ladybug," said Betsy. She brushed it off.

The house was creepy, all right. But it also had a sad, empty feeling to it.

Betsy shifted the books in her arms.

"Ida," she asked, "do . . . do you want me to help you?"

Ida wiped her brow. She looked at all the long grass, and her shoulders drooped.

But she shook her head.

"It's my project," she said in a low voice. "I said I'd do it, and I will."

Betsy and Julia walked home.

"Ida's too stubborn," said Julia.

"She never gives up," explained Betsy.

"Sometimes a person needs help," Julia said. "That's all there is to it."

An hour later Betsy looked out her window and saw Ida walking home.

Ida was holding her hands out in front of her. She walked so stiffly, it looked like she was pretending to be Frankenstein.

For a second Betsy was scared. Then she

realized Ida was tired and sore from working.

Betsy wished she could cheer her best friend up.

She had an idea.

The next morning she left for school early. No one was on the playground yet.

Betsy went straight to the willow tree. She picked up a long golden branch lying on the ground.

Humming happily, she got to work.

6

Red Is
for Danger

Later that morning, she read her Willow Report to the class.

"Trees were on earth long before people were," Betsy read. "Trees were here 300,000,000 years ago."

"Holy mackerel!" P.J. shouted out.

"P.J.," said Mrs. Myer sternly.

Betsy read on.

"Trees give the air oxygen. They vacuum dirt from the air."

P.J. made a noise like a vacuum.

"Willows are some of the fastest growing trees. Usually they grow where it is wet. So we are lucky to have one in our playground, which is almost a desert."

She was speaking up. She wasn't saying "umm" or "duh." Everyone in the class was listening carefully.

Almost everyone.

P.J. was tapping his nose and squinting out the window.

"Willows are used to make poles. And baskets. And paper. Plus they are beautiful."

"Hey," said P.J., "did you see . . ."

"Ssssh!" said Mrs. Myer.

"Weeping willows really come from China," Betsy read. "But people all over the world plant them in their yards."

Betsy folded up her paper. "Well," she said, "that's all for now."

Everyone started clapping. But Ida waved her hand.

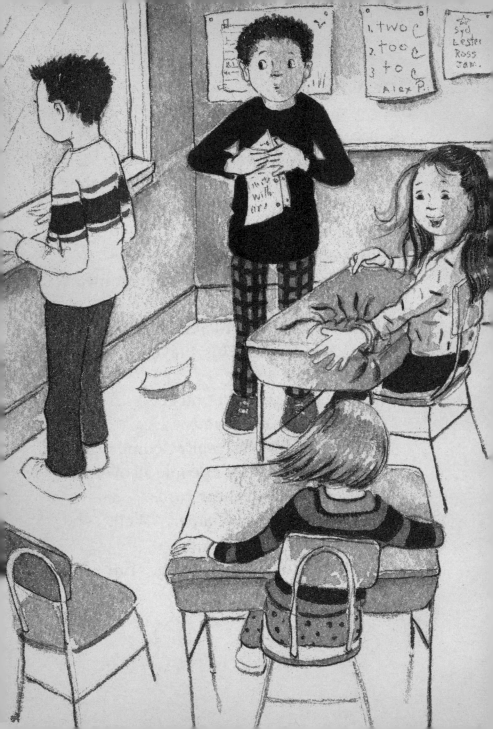

"Wait!" she cried. "That's NOT all!" She stuck out her arm.

"Willows are also used for making beautiful jewelry," she said proudly. On her arm was the golden bracelet Betsy had made her. She had bent two willow branches and woven them together.

Everyone was amazed.

"Can you make me one, Betsy?" Erin asked.

"Me, too!" said Tyler.

"Me three!"

"Me four!"

"Thank you for that excellent report, Betsy," said Mrs. Myer. "You've got us all going A.P.E. for the willow!"

P.J. was at the window. He turned around.

"Cool, Betsy," he said. "Cool as a penguin's belly."

"Huh?" said Betsy.

She walked over to the window.

The willow tree had red streamers flying from its branches.

Her heart skipped a beat.

"Where'd that come from?" she asked.

"You mean you didn't decorate it like that?" P.J. asked. "But who else would?"

"Hmmm," said Mrs. Myer. She looked out the window and frowned.

Betsy's heart beat faster.

Red was a warning color.

It was the color of danger.

Mrs. Myer was still frowning. She put her hand on Betsy's shoulder.

"An excellent report," she said again, and then she smiled. "Recess time!"

Outside, everyone crowded around the tree while Betsy made bracelets.

Once they saw how she did it, they started weaving things themselves. They made bracelets, anklets, necklaces, and crowns.

"Wow!" said Erin. "We look royal!"

"I'm the Queen of Sheba!" cried Ida.

"I'm the King of Siam!" said P.J.

They marched across the playground, yelling and laughing.

Only Betsy stayed behind.

Leaning against the willow, she watched the red streamers wave in the breeze.

She remembered how Mrs. Myer frowned when she saw them.

A willow branch touched her shoulder, as if it had a question to ask.

"I don't know," whispered Betsy. "I don't know what's going on."

7

The Red Van

Betsy could smell Missy before she saw her. She wrinkled her nose, and kept on writing.

"Hi, Bets." Missy came around the corner of the house. "Want some?" She held out her sauerkraut sandwich.

"No thanks," said Betsy. "Here, I made you this."

She gave Missy a willow bracelet, necklace, and ring.

"Gorgeous!" cried Missy. She put them

all on. "Are you still doing your willow report?"

"I'm doing another one. I . . . I left stuff out the first time."

Missy munched her sandwich. Her breath would knock over a skunk.

"Like what?" she asked.

"Like what a good back-scratcher it is. And how the branches do the hula. And how nice it sounds when the wind blows through it."

And how terrible those red streamers look, she thought.

Missy nodded. "You were smart to choose that tree. About three hundred times smarter than Ida."

"Poor Ida," said Betsy.

She closed her tree book. She was sick of worrying about the willow.

She stood up.

"Ida needs help," she told Missy. "I'm going to see what I can do."

Betsy told Julia where she was going.

She went down the block and around the corner.

Ida was sitting on the haunted house's broken-down steps.

Her head was in her hands. Her shoulders were jiggling.

Betsy stopped breathing.

Ida was crying her heart out.

"Ida!" Betsy rushed toward her. "Are you all right? Are you hurt?"

Ida looked up. She wiped her tears with the palms of her hands. She made a face.

"Ouch!" she squealed. "Ooh, ouch!"

"What?" cried Betsy. "Oh, Ida!"

This house really is haunted! she thought. *Something bad happened!*

Ida sniffled. "Look," she said. She held out her hands.

Her palms were fire red.

Her fingers had big white bumps.

"Blisters," said Ida. "From those dumb grass clippers."

34

"Rats," said Betsy. "Double rats."

"I can't work anymore," Ida said in a wobbly voice. "My hands hurt too much. I'm going to have to give up my project!"

Ida started crying again.

Betsy didn't know what to do.

Ida hardly ever cried. And she never, ever gave up.

"I'll help you," said Betsy. "I'll go get our clippers and . . ."

"It's no use," sobbed Ida. "It's too hard a job! How will I ever tell Mrs. Myer?"

Just then they heard a weird noise.

It sounded like a million tin cans clanking and clattering.

"Stand back!" someone shouted. "Look out!"

Missy came charging around the corner.

She was pushing an old-fashioned lawn mower. The kind with no engine.

"My dad said we could use it!" she cried. "As long as we keep our hands away from the blades!"

Missy pushed it up to the steps.

Ida raised her head.

"What's that smell? A sauerkraut factory?" she said. But she was smiling.

"Great idea, Missy Mason," she said. "But my hands are too sore to use the mower."

"I'll do it!" cried Missy. She started zooming around the yard.

"And I'll go get a broom and sweep the porch!" said Betsy.

"But . . . aren't you too scared to come near this house?" asked Ida.

"Not if I'm with you guys," said Betsy.

She ran home and got the broom.

She also got her mother's gardening gloves.

Ida put them on. She picked up candy wrappers and cans.

They were all working very hard, when a red van came down the street. As it passed the house, the van slowed down. It went so slowly, they all stopped working.

The van had tinted windows, so they couldn't see in.

But they could all tell someone was watching them.

Very slowly, the van turned the corner. Then suddenly the engine roared, and it sped out of sight.

"Woooeee!" said Missy. "I've got goose bumps all over."

"Me, too," whispered Betsy. "Who . . . or what . . . do you think it was?"

BANG!

Missy screamed.

Betsy started to run.

"Silly," said Ida. "It was only the broom falling over!"

She tried to sound calm. But her face was pale.

"Maybe this place really is haunted," said Missy. "Maybe the ghost of the old owner was driving that van."

"Yeah," said Betsy. "Maybe . . . maybe it was trying to scare us away!"

"Ridiculous," said Ida.

But she took off her work gloves.

"That's enough for today," she said.

They walked home without saying a word.

The only sound was Missy's lawn mower clanking.

At home Betsy went up to her room. Her cat Marbles was sleeping on her bed. Betsy sat down and petted him.

First the red streamers.

Now a spooky red van.

"Taking care of the earth is turning out to be hard," she told Marbles. "Maybe even dangerous."

But Marbles only went on sleeping.

8

Leave It
to Betsy

"And yesterday I planted baby cabbages and broccoli," said P.J.

He squeezed his eyes shut and hung his tongue out the side of his mouth.

"I hate cabbage and broccoli," he said. "But my grandma always plants them."

"Since *you* grew them, maybe you'll like them!" said Mrs. Myer.

"Yeah right," said P.J. "And maybe I'll be the first kid on the moon, too."

Everybody laughed.

P.J. was a wise guy. But they all liked him. Even Mrs. Myer.

"Thanks for your report on your project," she said. "Now it's Betsy's turn."

Mrs. Myer smiled at Betsy. But it wasn't her real smile.

It was a worried smile.

Betsy's heart skipped a beat. She dropped her paper.

She picked it up and tried to read. But her voice only croaked.

She tried again.

"Our willow tree is T.W.B.B.S.," she began. "That stands for The World's Best Back-Scratcher."

She read her whole report.

At the end she said, "When the first settlers came to North America, it was covered with gigantic forests. Trees were everyplace."

Her voice started croaking again. She cleared her throat.

"Here is what I am trying to say," she read. "The willow tree has more right to be here than we do. Thank you very much."

Betsy sat down.

Everyone clapped.

They were all wearing their willow jewelry.

"Hooray for Betsy," said Ida. "A.K.A. — that means Also Known As — Willow Woman!"

Mrs. Myer said, "Time for recess!"

But when Betsy started to line up, Mrs. Myer said, "Betsy, I need to talk to you."

The class went outside. Betsy and Mrs. Myer sat down.

Mrs. Myer was frowning.

Betsy's heart was beating hard.

"Betsy," said Mrs. Myer, "yesterday I went to talk to Mrs. Brown, the principal. I asked her about the willow."

Betsy bit her lip. She couldn't say a word.

"I have some bad news. They are going to cut the tree down."

Betsy jumped up from her seat. A big pile of papers hit the floor. She didn't care.

"They can't!" she cried. "It's mine! I mean, I adopted it. And . . ."

Mrs. Myer's face looked soft and sad.

"Willow trees have very long roots," she said. "The roots are growing into the drainage pipes underground. It's becoming a bad problem."

Mrs. Myer stood up. She put an arm around Betsy.

"I feel bad, too," she said. "I told Mrs. Brown how much the tree means to you."

"Not just me!" Betsy almost shouted. "The whole class loves that tree."

Mrs. Myer nodded. Her eyes were shiny.

"Mrs. Brown said maybe our class can plant another tree, farther away from the school."

Mrs. Myer walked Betsy to the door.

Outside, the class was making a big circle around the willow tree.

They held hands and danced around it.

"Oh dear," said Mrs. Myer. "Oh dear, oh dear, oh dear."

She looked down at Betsy.

"Who's going to tell them?" she asked. "You or me?"

Betsy thought for a minute.

"I will," she said at last. "But not yet, okay?"

"Okay," said Mrs. Myer with a sad smile. "I'll leave it up to you, Betsy."

9

The Darkest Afternoon

Betsy didn't tell anyone.

Not Missy, not Ida.

It was a windy afternoon. Dark clouds swept across the sky.

As soon as they got to the haunted house, Missy and Ida had a fight.

Ida wanted to knock down the spiderwebs on the front porch. Missy asked Ida how she would like it if someone knocked down her house.

The sky was getting darker.

46

Thunder rumbled in the distance.

Missy put a spider on Ida's arm.

Ida started shrieking and shaking her arm. Her arm knocked Missy in the head.

Missy stumbled against the porch railing.

The railing broke. Missy fell to the ground. She started to cry. LOUD.

Then they heard another sound.

A wail. LOUD.

"Woooeee!" cried Missy. "Hear that?"

"EEEE!" came the answer.

"It's just an echo," said Ida. "An echo of your dumb baby-crying!"

"It is not!" said Missy. She jumped to her feet.

"If you want to hang around a haunted house, go ahead! I'm getting out of here!"

Missy started for the sidewalk.

But then she froze.

The red van. They all saw it coming — slowly, ever so slowly, down the street.

Missy raced back. The three of them huddled together.

"I've got the grass clippers!" whispered Ida. "Just in case!"

"Rats!" whispered Betsy. "Double rats — it's stopping! What do we do now?"

The van's door swung open.

Someone very tall, dressed all in black, stepped out. A big hat shaded the person's face.

If it *was* a person.

"Just what do you kids think you're doing?" asked a loud, rough voice.

Nobody could speak. Not even Ida.

"Who gave you permission to mess with this house?" the voice demanded.

Missy hiccupped. She always got the hiccups when she was scared.

"What?" the voice asked.

A big hand pushed back the hat.

Betsy gasped. Missy hiccupped. Ida put her hands on her hips.

"You're just a teenager!" she said.

The teenager looked surprised. Then he scowled.

48

"You still didn't tell me what you're doing here!" he said.

"We're fixing up this house, that's what," said Ida. "No one takes care of it, so we adopted it."

"Did you ever hear of trespassing?" asked the teenager.

"Well," said Ida. "As a matter of fact . . . I mean . . ."

"It's against the law! If you didn't know it before, you do now!"

The teenager yanked his hat back over his eyes.

He got in his van and drove away fast.

"I'll bet he was a vampire in disguise," said Missy.

"Ridiculous," said Ida. "He was just a . . . a teenager showing off."

"Ida," said Betsy, "what if he's right?"

"What if we get — *hiccup!* — arrested?" Missy said.

Ida tossed her hair.

"I won't give up my project," she cried. "I WON'T!"

"Maybe you won't," Betsy burst out, "but I have to!"

Missy and Ida both stared at her.

Betsy couldn't keep the bad news inside any longer.

"Mrs. Myer says they're going to cut the willow down!"

10

Ida's Idea

It started to rain, but they hardly even noticed.

Betsy told them everything.

About the roots choking the pipes.

About the willow being cut down.

About planting another tree to take its place.

"That's ridiculous," said Ida. "It'll take forever for another tree to grow. We'll be all grown up by then!"

"Besides," said Missy, "no other tree

could ever be as sweet as that one."

Betsy's eyes felt hot. Her throat had a lump in it, like she'd taken too big a bite of something.

"I know," she said. The words just made it out over the lump.

"We have to do something," said Ida. She started pacing back and forth.

"Like what?" said Missy. "We're just kids. Nobody cares what we think."

"Remember what Mrs. Myer told us," said Ida.

She stopped pacing. She put a finger in the air. Her mouth made a shape like an egg.

She looked exactly like Mrs. Myer when she said *something important*.

"Remember, YOU can make a difference!" Ida said.

"I was trying," said Betsy sadly.

Rain was running down her neck and inside her shirt.

"I know!" cried Ida. "I have a brilliant idea!"

She twirled around.

"You think all your ideas are brilliant," complained Missy.

"We can have a protest!" Ida said.

"Woooeee!" said Missy. She looked excited.

"We can carry protest signs!" she said.

"We can lock hands around the tree!" Ida cried.

"And refuse to let go!" Missy said.

"Right!" said Ida. "Even when they bring the chain saws!"

"Chain saws? *Hiccup!*"

"To cut down the tree!" Ida crossed her arms on her chest. "We won't move even when the police come!"

"Police? *Hiccup!*"

"Right. We're already in trouble for trespassing. We might as well get in trouble for protesting, too."

Ida tossed her wet hair.

"I said I'd clean up this house. And Betsy said she'd take care of that tree." Ida threw an arm around Betsy. "We meant what we said! Right?"

Somehow, Betsy didn't think this was what Mrs. Myer had in mind. She didn't think Mrs. Myer meant for her students to wind up in jail.

Still, Betsy knew she'd do almost anything to save her tree.

"Right," she said.

"Let's get to work!"

"*Hiccup!*"

11

Protest!

Early Monday morning the three of them met by Betsy's garage.

They dragged out the big garbage bag hidden behind the old baby pool. Ida wanted to carry it by herself. But Missy said that wasn't fair.

"You aren't even in our class!" said Ida.

"So?" said Missy.

"Just take turns!" said Betsy.

She was very nervous. She didn't have the patience for one of Missy and Ida's fights.

"Me first," said Ida, lifting the bag.

By the time they got to school, a few kids were already on the playground.

"If you care about the earth, get over here!" Ida called to them.

She explained the plan.

Little by little, more kids arrived. They came over to see what was going on.

The youngest kids didn't understand. They ran off to play on the slide and swings.

Most of the big kids said the plan would never work. "Forget it," they said. "You might as well give up now."

But P.J. did a back flip.

"Cool! Cool as a polar bear's nose! Give me one right now!" he said.

He reached into the garbage bag and pulled out a piece of poster board.

KEEP OUR EARTH GREEN — SAVE THE WILLOW, it said.

Erin took one that said, GUESS WHAT? TREES GIVE US OXYGEN — SAVE THE WILLOW.

Tyler's said, WE NEED TREES AND
TREES NEED US — SAVE THE WILLOW.

Missy was hiccupping like crazy.

Betsy's knees felt wobbly, the way they
always did when she was angry or scared.

All she could think was, *What if this
doesn't work?*

The bell rang. Everyone ran to line up.

Everyone except Mrs. Myer's class, and
Missy.

Missy's sign said, TREES GIVE BUGS
HOMES — BIRDS AND ANIMALS TOO!

Circling the tree, they all held up their
signs.

Ida began to chant:

> *"Save the willow,*
> *Please, please, please!*
> *Save the earth,*
> *Keep our trees!"*

The other children joined in.

Their voices rose higher and higher.

They poked their signs up and down in the air.

Betsy hoped the willow didn't mind them making such a racket around it. She hoped the willow understood what they were doing.

"Just what do you think you're doing?"

Mrs. Myer came down the school steps. Her face looked jiggly, as if it couldn't decide to frown or smile.

Ida tossed her hair.

She held up her sign, which said:

IMAGINE A WORLD
WITHOUT TREES —
YUCK!

"We're having a peaceful protest, Mrs. Myer," she said. "And we would like to speak to the principal, please."

Mrs. Myer put a hand over her mouth.

Betsy hoped she wasn't going to faint.

But Mrs. Myer only turned and hurried back into the school.

"Keep on chanting!" ordered Ida.

"Save the willow!
Please, please, please!
Save the earth . . ."

"Woooeee," said Missy. "Look who's here!"

Mrs. Myer was coming toward them again.

Behind her marched the principal.

There was no question about whether she was smiling or frowning.

"Mrs. Brown is Mad City," said P.J.

"So!" said Mrs. Brown in her booming voice. "A peaceful protest! Who is your spokesperson?"

Everyone looked at Ida. But Ida gave Betsy a little push.

"Go on," she whispered.

Betsy couldn't believe it. Ida always wanted to be in charge.

"You love this tree more than anyone," Ida whispered. "Go for it!"

Betsy stumbled forward.

She held her sign against her chest.

Her sign had no words.

It was just a picture of the willow with a big heart around it.

"Betsy Jones?" said Mrs. Brown. "I'm waiting to hear what you have to say."

She crossed her arms on her chest.

A million different words tumbled in Betsy's head.

How was she supposed to know which ones were the right ones? The ones that would make Mrs. Brown change her mind?

Then she saw Mrs. Myer looking at her.

Mrs. Myer gave a little nod.

Betsy opened her mouth.

"We . . . we want to make a difference," she croaked.

"You're upset about the tree being cut down!" boomed Mrs. Brown. "But it's become a nuisance."

"The willow is the only tree on the whole playground. If you cut it down, the playground will be ugly and hot," Betsy said.

"If we leave it, it will damage our pipes! What do you have to say about that?"

Betsy looked down at the ground.

"I don't know," she said.

"You have to see both sides of a problem," boomed Mrs. Brown.

Betsy kept looking at the ground.

She saw the tips of Mrs. Brown's shoes. They were pointy and brown. Ugly.

Then she heard Mrs. Myer's voice.

"You're right, Mrs. Brown," said Mrs. Myer. "And I have an idea."

Betsy looked up. She was holding her sign so tight, her hands were all sweaty. Marker was coming off all over her fingers.

"My neighbor had a problem with roots in her pipes," said Mrs. Myer. "Instead of cutting down the tree, she had someone come to cut the roots."

"But that will kill the tree!" cried P.J.

Mrs. Myer shook her head.

"They only cleaned out the ones in the pipes. The tree was fine," she said.

"The roots will just grow back," said Mrs. Brown. "The school can't afford to keep cutting them."

"But," said Betsy, "you can't replace that willow. Not for all the money in the world."

"She's right," said Ida.

"One hundred per cent," said P.J.

"Woooeee," whispered Missy.

They all started chanting again.

*"Save the willow,
Please, please, please!"*

Mrs. Brown uncrossed her arms.
Then she crossed them again.
She looked at Mrs. Myer.
Mrs. Myer smiled.

Mrs. Brown shook her head and smiled back.

"Well," Mrs. Brown said. "I'll have to think about this."

"Thank you very much, Mrs. Brown," said Mrs. Myer.

And then, with that jiggly look on her face, she led the class inside.

12

Return to the
Haunted House

That whole day went by, and Mrs. Brown didn't tell them her decision.

Then another day.

Then another.

Every time the classroom door opened, Betsy jumped.

But each time it was only a kid. Or another teacher. Or someone's mother.

Never Mrs. Brown.

On Thursday Mrs. Myer asked them to draw new pictures of their A.P.E. projects.

"Let's see if you've made a difference," she said.

P.J. drew the new plants coming up in neat, green rows in his grandmother's garden.

Tyler drew his bus stop. Marigolds were popping up in the flowerpots he had put there.

Erin drew the alley by her apartment. "See?" she said. "Not a single speck of litter."

Betsy drew the willow, with the red streamers on it.

"It reminds me of a turkey on the day before Thanksgiving," said Ida gloomily. "It has no idea what's coming."

Ida did a messy drawing of the haunted house.

They hadn't been back to it once, since the teenager yelled at them.

Mrs. Myer looked over Ida's shoulder.

"What's wrong, Ida?" she asked. "You

were so excited about your project."

Ida shrugged. She tossed her hair.

Betsy could tell she was miserable.

"What's this big red shape in the corner of your drawing?" Mrs. Myer asked.

"Just a van passing by," said Ida. "Nothing important."

Betsy coughed very loud. But Ida didn't look at her.

After school Betsy said, "Ida, let's go work on the haunted house."

Ida's eyes went wide.

"You really want to?" she said. "I thought you didn't want to anymore. And Missy's too chicken-hearted to go back there."

"I heard that!"

Missy came stomping over. A huge pink worm dangled from one hand. She had just rescued it from a puddle.

"Who are you calling chicken, Ida Rose?"

She dangled the worm in front of Ida's face.

Ida took a big step back. She looked a little sick.

"Quit wasting time, Missy Mason," she said. "We need to get to work A.S.A.P. That means . . ."

"I know!" shouted Missy. "As Soon As Possible."

They ran down the street.

But the closer they got to the house, the slower they ran. By the time they got to the corner, they were just walking.

And then, as they turned the corner, they saw it.

Parked right out front.

The red van.

Red, the color of danger.

Ida grabbed Betsy's hand. Betsy grabbed Missy's.

I won't stop until Ida does, thought Betsy.

Ida kept on going.

Missy started hiccupping.

Betsy's feet had boulders attached to them. She could hardly pick them up.

"Woooeee," whispered Missy. "This time the vampire brought someone with him!"

13

The Girls
from M.A.D.

They hid behind a big, raggedy bush and spied.

The teenager was standing on the broken-down porch. He was talking to a short man with wispy white hair.

"A wizard!" whispered Missy.

"SSSHHH!" said Ida.

The teenager looked around.

He jumped down off the porch, and started walking toward them.

The white-haired man called to him.

The teenager looked back.

Betsy saw the tree root sticking up out of the grass.

But the teenager didn't.

Splat! He was flat on his face.

His left hand was on Ida's shoe.

"What the . . ." he said.

Ida stepped out from behind the bush.

"If you try to arrest us, I demand to see a lawyer," she said.

The teenager sat up. He rubbed his knees. He looked disgusted.

"Granddad!" he yelled. "Over here!"

The man with the white hair came toward them.

His face was round and pink, like Santa's. He looked at Ida with dark, curious eyes.

"This is one of them," the teenager said grumpily. "The other two are hiding in the bush."

The man peered into the bush.

"Just exactly what are you girls up to?" asked the man.

"Hiccup!" hiccupped Missy.

"Urk," croaked Betsy.

"We're . . . we're from M.A.D.," said Ida. "That stands for Make A Difference."

The man stroked his chin.

"I see," he said.

"Our mission is to fix up this haunted . . . I mean, this house."

"So my grandson told me." The man looked at the teenager, who rolled his eyes.

"This is my house," said the man. "It's the house I was born in. After I grew up and moved away, my parents went on living here."

"We never saw anybody live here," said Ida.

"They've both been dead for a long time," said the man.

"Hiccup!"

"My job was in another city," the man said. "So I couldn't live here. I should have sold the house, but . . ."

The man rubbed his chin.

"I couldn't bring myself to do it," he went on. "I have too many happy memories of living here."

"Are your parents the ghosts of the house?" asked Missy.

"Ghosts?" said the man. He peered into the bush.

"Everybody says the house is haunted," Missy explained.

"I told you they were loony, Granddad," said the teenager.

"The house isn't haunted," the man said sadly. "It's just neglected."

"It needs T.L.C.," said Ida.

The man nodded.

"Right," he said. "I didn't have the money to take care of the house. I let it get run-down. That was a mistake."

"Don't feel so bad, Granddad," said the teenager.

He kicked a rusty can with his black boot. Then he put an arm around the old man's shoulder.

"Bobby here knows how much this house means to me," the man said. "That's why he scolded you the other day."

"We were only trying to help," said Ida.

The man nodded again.

"I know. And you have helped. When Bobby told me about you, I started thinking."

The man drew a deep breath.

"Today I decided to do something," he said.

He smiled. A million lines crinkled his face. Now he really looked like Santa.

"I'm going to get a loan. I'll get the house fixed up, the way it used to be. Then maybe I can rent it to a nice family."

The man held out his hand.

"You girls made me start thinking," he said. "It's because of you I'm doing this. Thank you."

"On behalf of M.A.D., you're welcome," Ida said.

She shook his hand.

Missy and Betsy came out of the bush and shook his hand.

The teenager rolled his eyes again.

But then he held out his hand, too.

14

Mrs. Brown Decides

The next day Ida could hardly wait to tell the class the news.

Everyone was amazed.

Ida tossed her long, beautiful hair.

She did a little twirl.

Then she looked across the room at Betsy.

"I couldn't have done it without Betsy," Ida said.

Betsy tried to smile.

She was happy about the haunted house.

She really was.

But today was Friday.

If Mrs. Brown didn't decide today, Betsy would have to wait the whole weekend.

Why was the principal taking so long to make up her mind? Was that a good sign or a bad sign?

Betsy had no idea.

She tried to work on her math. But she made so many mistakes, she erased a hole in the paper.

She almost never did that anymore.

"Rats," she sighed. "Double rats."

She got up for a new piece of paper.

And then the classroom door opened.

In walked Mrs. Brown.

She whispered something to Mrs. Myer.

Betsy was amazed that Mrs. Brown could whisper. All she had ever heard Mrs. Brown do was boom.

"Boys and girls," said Mrs. Myer, "please come up to the front of the room."

Ida practically sat on top of Betsy. Betsy smelled the bubble gum toothpaste Ida had used that morning.

"This is it," Ida hissed.

She grabbed Betsy's hand. The blisters on Ida's palm felt like little leather bumps.

"Listen up, class!" said Mrs. Brown.

Now she *was* booming. Indoors, her voice sounded bigger than ever.

"I've been working on our problem," she said. "I called a company about cleaning out the pipes. As I guessed, it would be expensive."

Ida squeezed Betsy's hand so tight, it felt like the bones were moving around inside.

"However," Mrs. Brown said.

She stopped. She looked straight down at Betsy and Ida.

"However," Mrs. Brown went on, "it would not be nearly as expensive as removing such a large tree."

She kept looking at Betsy and Ida.

"Betsy," she said finally, "you look like

you're going to cry. Don't you understand what I'm telling you?"

"Ida's killing my hand," explained Betsy. "Do you mean . . ."

"I mean, you made a difference!" boomed Mrs. Brown.

Her eyes twinkled. "We'll spare that old tree, at least for now."

The class went crazy.

"We did it! We did it!" they shouted.

"Listen up!" boomed Mrs. Brown.

"I can't promise we will NEVER have to remove it," she said. "But for now, your efforts have paid off. I congratulate you."

"Mrs. Brown?" said Betsy.

"Yes, Betsy?"

"Can I . . . is it okay if we take those streamers off now?"

"Special recess!" Mrs. Brown announced. "Everyone line up nicely!"

But Betsy couldn't wait.

She ducked out the door and ran straight to the tree.

She pulled off the streamers and stuffed them in the garbage.

Then she leaned her back against the trunk.

She rubbed her shoulders up and down, up and down.

All around her, the branches swayed and danced.

One touched her lightly on the shoulder, as if it wanted to tell her something.

"Oh," said Betsy, "you're very welcome."

Now the rest of the class came charging out.

Some of them held hands and danced around the tree.

Some of them started weaving jewelry.

P.J. was yelling, "We saved the tree! Yes siree!"

Suddenly Missy came shooting out the door. She was holding her fingers in a V for Victory.

"I saw you out the window! My teacher said I could come out, too. Wooeee!"

Missy gave Betsy and Ida the high five.

Then she threw her arms around the willow.

"Hey, I've got a new one," said Betsy. "H.O.T."

"What does it stand for?" Ida asked.

"Hug Our Tree!" answered Betsy.

And they did.

About the Author

When Tricia Springstubb was growing up, she spent many happy days playing "pioneers" and "ranch" in the big open field behind her house. She still remembers how sad she was when houses were built on the field, changing it forever. It was this memory, along with her daughters' love of the willow trees that grow on their school playground, that made her write *Two Plus One Goes A.P.E.*

Plus, she really believes we can all make a difference!

Tricia Springstubb lives in Cleveland Heights, Ohio, with her husband, three girls, and two cats. This is her third book about Betsy, Missy, and Ida.